Copy Cat

John Mole

Illustrated by Bee Willey

Kingfisher

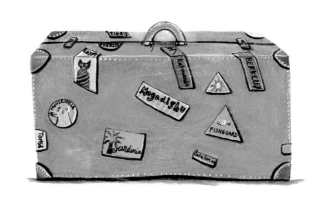

One morning when Oliver woke up...

he found a strange cat sitting at the bottom of his bed.

It was looking at him in a funny sort of way.

When Oliver went into the bathroom to brush his teeth
the cat did too.

When Oliver poured the milk on to his cornflakes
the cat did too.

When Oliver played with his bricks
the cat did too.

When Oliver wanted to watch television
the cat did too.

television

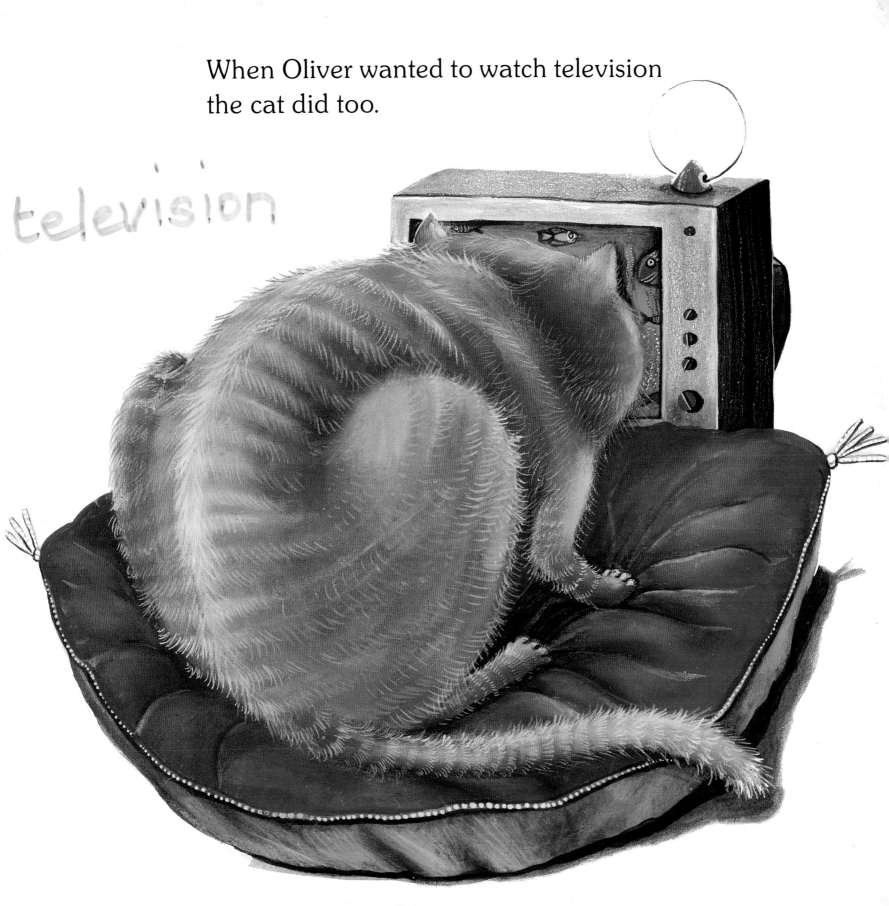

When Oliver tried to eat his dinner the cat did too.

dinner

When Oliver wondered what to do next
the cat did too.

When Oliver invited his friends to tea the cat did too.

friends

When Oliver started to clear up the mess
the cat did too.

Then Oliver said,
"This just won't do!
If you copy me
I'll copy you."   So…

When the cat washed behind its ears
Oliver did too.

washed

When the cat found a snug and secret place
Oliver did too.

When the cat pretended to sleep
Oliver did too.

sleep

When the cat jumped up on to the table
Oliver did too.

When the cat made a fuss and wanted to be let out Oliver did too.

When the cat decided to go hunting
Oliver did too.

When the cat found a special friend
Oliver did too.

When both cats danced in the moonlight
Oliver did too.

Then the cat thought,
"This won't do!
If you don't copy me
I won't copy you."

And that was that.

Next morning when Oliver woke up,
he found a strange dog sitting
at the bottom of his bed.

He looked at it in a *very* funny sort of way.